The Witch with an Itch

Helen Baugh

Deborah Allwright

JONATHAN CAPE · LONDON

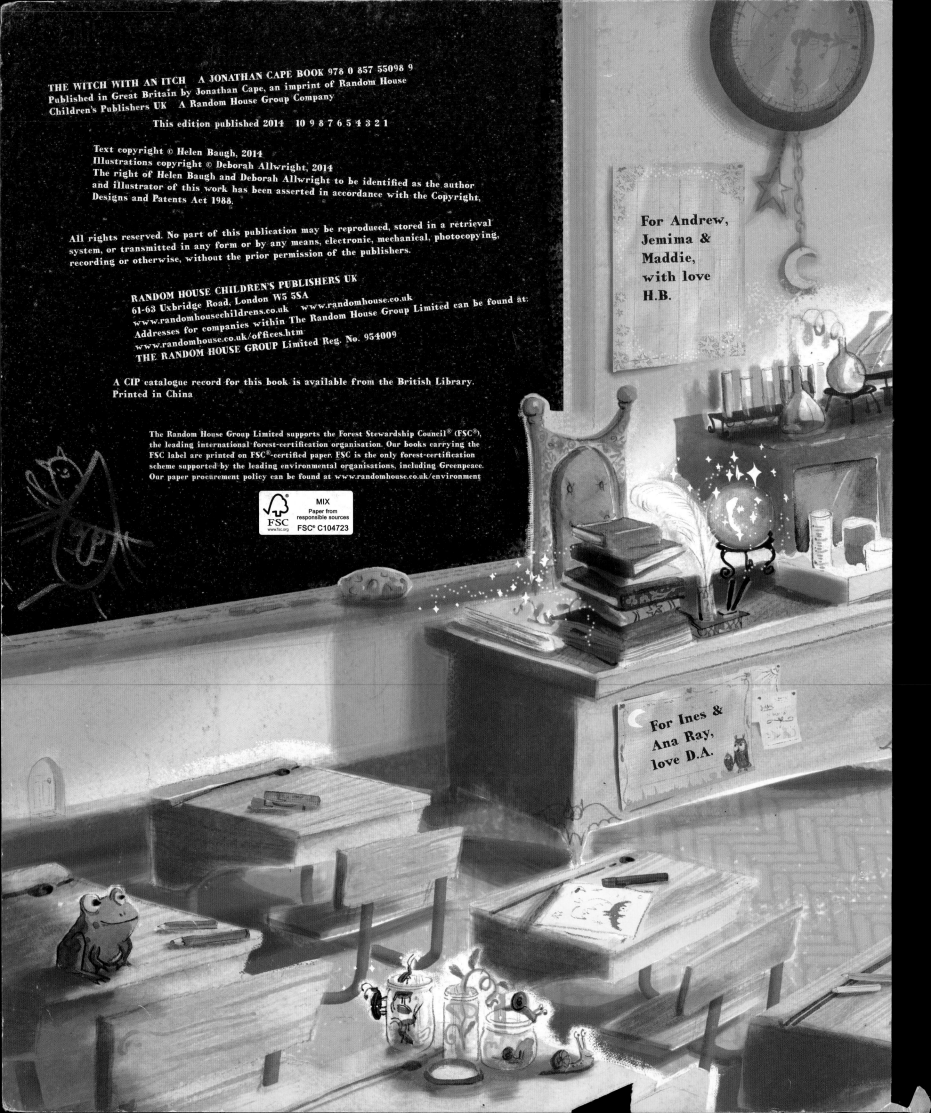

THE WITCH WITH AN ITCH   A JONATHAN CAPE BOOK 978 0 857 55098 9
Published in Great Britain by Jonathan Cape, an imprint of Random House
Children's Publishers UK   A Random House Group Company

This edition published 2014   10 9 8 7 6 5 4 3 2 1

Text copyright © Helen Baugh, 2014
Illustrations copyright © Deborah Allwright, 2014
The right of Helen Baugh and Deborah Allwright to be identified as the author
and illustrator of this work has been asserted in accordance with the Copyright,
Designs and Patents Act 1988.

RANDOM HOUSE CHILDREN'S PUBLISHERS UK
61-63 Uxbridge Road, London W5 5SA
www.randomhousechildrens.co.uk   www.randomhouse.co.uk
Addresses for companies within The Random House Group Limited can be found at:
www.randomhouse.co.uk/offices.htm
THE RANDOM HOUSE GROUP Limited Reg. No. 954009

A CIP catalogue record for this book is available from the British Library.
Printed in China

The Random House Group Limited supports the Forest Stewardship Council® (FSC®),
the leading international forest-certification organisation. Our books carrying the
FSC label are printed on FSC®-certified paper. FSC is the only forest-certification
scheme supported by the leading environmental organisations, including Greenpeace.
Our paper procurement policy can be found at www.randomhouse.co.uk/environment

FSC
www.fsc.org

MIX
Paper from
responsible sources
FSC® C104723

For Andrew,
Jemima &
Maddie,
with love
H.B.

For Ines &
Ana Ray,
love D.A.

On the last day of witch school
the littlest witch . . .

Little Witch Academy

... passed her witchy exams
with not one
single hitch.

"Hurray!"
she exclaimed as she started to run.
"At last I am free for some
mischief and fun!"

The first thing she saw (looking slimy and cool)
was a frog on a rock at the side of a pool.

"Ho ho!" thought the witch as she got into place,
with a gleam in her eye and a grin on her face.
"I've learned all my magic,
I know what to do.
Now I will try out
my first spell on

YOU!

"Hubble and bubble
and spittety-spat.
It's time for a change.
Now turn into a hat!"

BUT . . .

. . . the witch got an itch as the last word was said and pointed her wand at a flower instead.

"Something's gone wrong!"
said the witch to the cat.

**"The frog hasn't changed.
And where is the hat?"**

The next thing she saw as she went on her way
was a spider, spinning her web for the day.

"Oh my!" thought the witch as she got into place,
with some doubt in her eye
and a frown on her face.
"I've practised for years,
I should know what to do.
Now I will try out
my next spell on

YOU!

Hubble and bubble
and flippety-floom.
It's time for a change.

Now
turn
into
a
broom!"

BUT . . .

. . . the witch got an itch
as the last word was said

and pointed her wand
at a toadstool instead.

"No!" cried the witch
in a voice full of doom.

**"The spider's still here.
And where is the broom?"**

The next thing she saw
        (peering this way and that)
was a newt in the shade
            looking shiny and fat.

"Oh bats!" thought the witch
    as she got into place,
with a fire in her eye and a rage on her face.
"If this doesn't work, I won't know what to do.
Now I will try out
    my last spell on

YOU!

"Hubble and bubble and spittety-spot.

It's time for a change.

Now turn into a pot!"

BUT . . .

. . . the witch got an itch
as the last word was said
and pointed her wand
at a big stone instead.

The cat couldn't look and the witch lost the plot.
**"The newt's stayed the same!
And where is the pot?"**

"THAT'S IT!!"

screamed the witch (going red in the face),
with no hint of calmness, composure or grace.

"I've tried to be patient **but that's the last straw!**"
And she threw her new wand down with force on the floor.

"It's not me going wrong!
It's this wand –
it's no good!
It just doesn't work
like a magic wand
should!"

Then all of a sudden
the little witch spied
a girl with a hat,
pot and broom by her side.

"I believe these are yours," said the girl to the witch.
"And I think I know why you keep getting an itch.
It's not the wand's fault – I'm afraid that it's you.
Would you like me to say what I think you should do?"

The witch thought about it (but not for too long).
"Please tell me," she said, "why my spells all go wrong."

The girl cried, "It's easy! Haven't you guessed?
You're not a bad witch. You are one of the best!
You're allergic to bad spells, you're good through and through.
That's why only good spells will work out for you."

"Only **GOOD** spells?" hissed the witch in a huff.

"Are you bats?

Are you bonkers?

I've heard enough."

"Wait!" begged the girl. "Forget mischief and trouble.
There's no need to bother with hubble and bubble.

Please think of
the spider,
the frog and
the newt . . .

. . . I know they're not fluffy or cuddly or cute.

But they have their own lives and like them a lot,
so it's not fair to change them to things they are not.

Just think up new spells that don't hurt anyone,
    then your magic will work
    and your itch
        will be
        gone."

The witch's mind started to whir and to whirl
as she thought it all over, then said to the girl:

"If you're right then at last I will know what to do.
So now I will try out my new spell on

YOU!

Hobble and bobble and tickety-tock.

Please turn that dress into a fancy new frock!"

The spell worked like magic!

The witch did not itch!

The girl's frock was perfect,
down to the last stitch.

And from that
moment onwards
they played every day,

having fun with good spells . . .

. . . and the itch went away.